SANTA AND THE PIRATE QUEEN

A SAILING ROMANCE STORY

M. L. BUCHMAN

PRAISE FOR M. L. BUCHMAN

A fabulous soaring thriller.

> — *TAKE OVER AT MIDNIGHT*, MIDWEST
> BOOK REVIEW

Meticulously researched, hard-hitting, and suspenseful.

> — *PURE HEAT*, PUBLISHERS WEEKLY,
> STARRED REVIEW

Expert technical details abound, as do realistic military missions with superb imagery that will have readers feeling as if they are right there in the midst and on the edges of their seats.

> — *LIGHT UP THE NIGHT*, RT REVIEWS, 4
> 1/2 STARS

Buchman has catapulted his way to the top tier of my favorite authors.

> — FRESH FICTION

Nonstop action that will keep readers on the edge of their seats.

— *TAKE OVER AT MIDNIGHT*, LIBRARY JOURNAL

M L. Buchman's ability to keep the reader right in the middle of the action is amazing.

— LONG AND SHORT REVIEWS

The only thing you'll ask yourself is, "When does the next one come out?"

— *WAIT UNTIL MIDNIGHT*, RT REVIEWS, 4 STARS

The first...of (a) stellar, long-running (military) romantic suspense series.

— *THE NIGHT IS MINE*, BOOKLIST, "THE 20 BEST ROMANTIC SUSPENSE NOVELS: MODERN MASTERPIECES"

I knew the books would be good, but I didn't realize how good.

— NIGHT STALKERS SERIES, KIRKUS REVIEWS

Buchman mixes adrenalin-spiking battles and brusque military jargon with a sensitive approach.

— PUBLISHERS WEEKLY

13 times "Top Pick of the Month"

— NIGHT OWL REVIEWS

Tom Clancy fans open to a strong female lead will clamor for more.

— *DRONE*, PUBLISHERS WEEKLY

Superb! Miranda is utterly compelling!

— *BOOKLIST,* STARRED REVIEW

Miranda Chase continues to astound and charm.

— BARB M.

Escape Rating: A. Five Stars! OMG just start with *Drone* and be prepared for a fantastic binge-read!

— READING REALITY

The best military thriller I've read in a very long time. Love the female characters.

SIGN UP FOR M. L. BUCHMAN'S NEWSLETTER TODAY

and receive:
Release News
Free Short Stories
a Free Book

Get your free book today. Do it now.
free-book.mlbuchman.com

Other works by M. L. Buchman: *(* - also in audio)*

Action-Adventure Thrillers

Dead Chef
One Chef!
Two Chef!

Miranda Chase
Drone*
Thunderbolt*
Condor*
Ghostrider*
Raider*
Chinook*
Havoc*
White Top*
Start the Chase*
Lightning*

Science Fiction / Fantasy

Deities Anonymous
Cookbook from Hell: Reheated
Saviors 101

Single Titles
Monk's Maze
the Me and Elsie Chronicles

Contemporary Romance

Eagle Cove
Return to Eagle Cove
Recipe for Eagle Cove
Longing for Eagle Cove
Keepsake for Eagle Cove

Love Abroad
Heart of the Cotswolds: England
Path of Love: Cinque Terre, Italy

Where Dreams
Where Dreams are Born
Where Dreams Reside
Where Dreams Are of Christmas*
Where Dreams Unfold
Where Dreams Are Written
Where Dreams Continue

Non-Fiction

Strategies for Success
Managing Your Inner Artist/Writer
Estate Planning for Authors*
Character Voice
Narrate and Record Your Own
Audiobook*

Short Story Series by M. L. Buchman:

Action-Adventure Thrillers

Dead Chef
Miranda Chase Origin Stories

Romantic Suspense

Antarctic Ice Fliers
US Coast Guard

Contemporary Romance

Eagle Cove

Other

Deities Anonymous (fantasy)
Single Titles

The Emily Beale Universe
(military romantic suspense)

The Night Stalkers
MAIN FLIGHT
The Night Is Mine
I Own the Dawn
Wait Until Dark
Take Over at Midnight
Light Up the Night
Bring On the Dusk
By Break of Day
Target of the Heart
Target Lock on Love
Target of Mine
Target of One's Own
NIGHT STALKERS HOLIDAYS
Daniel's Christmas*
Frank's Independence Day*
Peter's Christmas*
Christmas at Steel Beach
Zachary's Christmas*
Roy's Independence Day*
Damien's Christmas*
Christmas at Peleliu Cove

Henderson's Ranch
Nathan's Big Sky*
Big Sky, Loyal Heart*
Big Sky Dog Whisperer*
Tales of Henderson's Ranch*

Shadow Force: Psi
At the Slightest Sound*
At the Quietest Word*
At the Merest Glance*
At the Clearest Sensation*

White House Protection Force
Off the Leash*
On Your Mark*
In the Weeds*

Firehawks
Pure Heat
Full Blaze
Hot Point*
Flash of Fire*
Wild Fire
SMOKEJUMPERS
Wildfire at Dawn*
Wildfire at Larch Creek*
Wildfire on the Skagit*

Delta Force
Target Engaged*
Heart Strike*
Wild Justice*
Midnight Trust*

Emily Beale Universe Short Story Series

The Night Stalkers
The Night Stalkers Stories
The Night Stalkers CSAR
The Night Stalkers Wedding Stories
The Future Night Stalkers

Delta Force
Th Delta Force Shooters
The Delta Force Warriors

Firehawks
The Firehawks Lookouts
The Firehawks Hotshots
The Firebirds

White House Protection Force
Stories

Future Night Stalkers
Stories (Science Fiction)

ABOUT THIS BOOK

AGAINST ALL BOUNDS OF COMMON SENSE, JANINE LANDS herself in charge of her yacht club's annual Christmas Potluck. Sailing the tricky course between a clean finish and a complete wreck, she desperately needs a rescue. Or perhaps it's time to set her own course.

Howie loves to sail but saving to buy his own boat takes time. He volunteers as crew when he can. And for the annual whirl of yacht club parties, he gate crashes as Santa.

When he sees one club has declared a pirate theme, he can't resist and goes in with full sails set.

But neither of them expect to find love in Santa's gift bag.

1

THE WIND GUSTED PAST SIXTY KNOTS OUT OF THE WEST-northwest. Not an issue from any other point of the compass, but WNW winds slid past the marina's breakwater, took a stroll down the lane between T and U docks, and hammered into slip T19.

Her slip.

Anything over forty-seven knots made her boat bob and weave like a drunk penguin.

"November storms suck!" Janine yelled at the boat. Ship's Captain Master Howl opened one eye, rolled onto his back and began to purr, forcing Janine to rub his furry black belly. Not as if she could do anything else. Her forty-one-foot Cheoy Lee sailboat, *Tārā*, twisted badly enough that she was far more likely to type *Gwko~* than *Help!* or *Sthj@* than *ARGH!* as the laptop slid one way and her fingers went the other.

Giving it up, she slapped the cover closed and tucked it into the drawer under the chart table. Scooping up Master Howl in her arms, Janine staggered forward—

banging a shoulder against the starboard door to the head, almost dropping Master Howl as she crashed her hip against the cooktop in the portside galley, and finally shuffled fast enough to plummet into the starboard-most seat of C-shaped settee rather than plunging into the closet.

The settee was the oddest feature of the Cheoy Lee's design, but one she'd come to love. Most boats would have two sofa seats with some awkward arrangement to raise a table in the middle of the aisle when guests and meals were happening. Her boat had a circular sofa that could seat eight. The mouth of the C-shape opened to the stern to either side of where the mast punched through on its way to the keel. A fold-up table hung from the back of the mast.

She shuffled around the seat until the two of them were ensconced in the backmost position. This part of the seat could be folded aside to access the forward cabin, which she rarely used except for sail storage. Once seated on the centerline of the boat, the action felt much less violent, now no more than a gentle rocking. Books flopped side-to-side on the shelf with a gentle slap. Spice bottles rattled against each other in the galley. Miscellaneous gear clanked to one side then another in the various storage cubbies. And though she couldn't hear the water sloshing about in the bilge, she could hear the pump engage and shut down as it was alternately submerged and exposed with the rolling of the boat.

All the sounds of home. Then a blast of rain and hail pounded on the deck over her head, drumming like an all-percussion marching band.

"Gonna be a long night, Master Howl."

He answered with an orca-sized yawn as befit his black coat and white chest patch. Though his hair fell more into the shaggy category than the sleek and dangerous one.

He *had* been a howler as a kitten but age had mellowed him. It was now far easier to picture him snoozing in a rope coil, sipping a White Russian (without the vodka or Kahlúa diluting the cream, of course), and occasionally rousing himself to batter his catnip toy crew into submission. It made him the perfect ship's captain. Though he still did occasionally give full voice to his discontent—especially if his dinner was more than three seconds late. He considered her ignoring that while navigating tricky archipelago passages to be grounds for mutiny. She had taught him quickly enough that batting her with his claws out counted as a gross breach of the ship's articles under which she served.

Of course it was better than being saddled with a dog. She'd trust Joshua Slocum on that point. On sailing the first solo circumnavigation of the globe in the 1890s, he'd considered taking on a local to help him pass through the Strait of Magellan. But the man had insisted that no one in their right mind would attempt that passage without a *doog* on board. Per his book *Sailing Alone Around the World*, Slocum *drew the line at dogs*. Janine had cleaved to that advice and never regretted her decision to do so.

Here, at the centerline with a warm cat in her arms, and the boat rocking side-to-side like the perfect cradle for a grown woman, she wanted to fall asleep. She really did. She tried.

Master Howl succeeded easily enough.

But her? Oh no! Tomorrow was *her* day and it wouldn't stop churning up a turbulent wake in her head.

With kind words and the hints of how much fun it would be, the secretary-general of the local yacht club had suckered her into organizing the annual Christmas Sailor's Potluck. A crime for which she'd never forgive him.

The reality had no relation to the purported ease and fun.

The other volunteers' expectations were that they could have everything exactly their way, that it was fully under their control, and that the louder they protested the more likely they would succeed.

However, Janine had been sailing far too long to be fooled. Everyone who had ever skippered a boat, even an eight-foot rubber dinghy, would gladly don a t-shirt declaring *I'm the Captain so, of course, I'm right!* She tried not to wince at the one in her own collection stating *I'm the Captain. Rule #1: The Captain is always right. Rule #2: Any questions? See Rule #1.*

Organizing a potluck should be merely sending out a few fun invites and reminders. A little bit of dish coordination so that not *everyone* brings a package of QFC chocolate chip cookies, and make up a few fun door prizes.

Except Georgina Anne wanted there to be fixed seating and a size limit.

Michael wanted to turn it into a fifty-dollar-a-head fundraiser (that Janine was sure was actually to keep the riff-raff like herself out but that Georgina Anne took personally).

Bethany had organized a decorating committee with her two BFFs, and they'd wanted a committed budget several times the yacht club's annual membership fee.

This wasn't the Seattle Yacht Club costing tens of thousands of dollars with thirty-six-month payment plans (for those in need). Nor was it the Sloop Tavern Yacht Club with a ninety-dollar fee, which also registered your boat for all of their races. She'd chosen one that cost in the hundreds—after having broken up with the head barman at the Sloop, which had definitely cancelled her prior membership there. Danny had been cool about it, but not the patrons.

The Lakefront Yacht Club landed in the casual zone between the two. A little upscale from the guys chugging pints at the start of a race no matter what the hour. It made for a nice change. Except the LYC also gathered all of the wannabes who the Seattle Yacht Club would never allow on their clubhouse verandah much less as members. And the worst of the lot had harangued her hourly on every social media platform known to womankind.

Finally sick of them all, she'd issued the invite to the full membership for the Annual Christmas *Pirate's* Potluck, set a suggested door price of a wrapped present for a homeless kid, and called it done. Once out, no one had the balls to take it back. When Bethany and her BFFs had attempted to vote her out, she'd invoked the *I'm-the-Captain* rule. Finally, the club's secretary-general had backed her up over Bethany's protests with a simple email: *Janine's the organizer*. Three whole words from a man who typically communicated in story-length volumes.

Tomorrow would either be immense fun. Or—

"Worst they can do is keelhaul me, right, Master Howl?"

On a particularly rough buck of the boat, her cat rolled out of her arms to plop into her lap, more like a beanbag than a cat with an actual skeleton somewhere beneath all that fur.

Janine sighed and began beating the back of her head against the partition that separated the settee from the forward stateroom. Not hard enough to knock herself out, though the thought did come to mind.

2

HOWIE LIEBERMANN LOVED CHRISTMAS. OR AT LEAST THE Christmas season. Mom loved having the annual *Hanukkah bush* in the living room. Dad always turned surly for a week or so after its arrival before caving in. It was hard to blame him. Each year he caught hell from Grandma when she visited, which seemed unfair as Jews didn't go in for the whole Hell thing—more of a Limbo-like retraining center for souls destined to enter the Garden of Eden on high.

Howie and his two sisters could always count on the worst presents under the Menorah. How many wooden dreidels and cheap milk chocolate wrapped in gold foil did three kids need after all? Grandma's Fifth Night gelt always eased the pain a little. The five-dollar *fortune* they'd received as little kids had never crossed twenty even in the lean college years. She paid their tuitions—her and Grandpa's sewing machine business had been very successful—but never more than a twenty on Fifth Night. The best presents always landed *under* the

Hanukkah bush—which they had trimmed with twinkle lights and eclectic ornaments. Presents that just happened to be opened on December 25th, though nothing from Grandma, of course.

That wasn't why he loved Christmas.

His passion for the holiday season had sprung into being when he'd escaped Brooklyn under the impetus of a cool job and cruised into Seattle's land of year-round sailing.

And the best part about Christmas here was definitely the great sailing parties and races. The Seattle Yacht Club Championships close before Halloween, typically coincident with the Sloop Tavern's Great Pumpkin Race at the other end of the spectrum. The Turkey Bowl race that the Corinthian Yacht Club on the Friday after Thanksgiving. Again, the Sloop's Dark & Stormy Christmas Light Cruise (and inevitable after-party). All the nights with parades of Christmas boats along different sections of Seattle's vast waterfronts were illumination spectacles.

And every club had an annual Christmas potluck.

Howie had never joined any of the clubs, though he'd enjoyed the round of *Introduction* dinners every club offered as they sought new members. Instead, he'd made a small name for himself on the local race circuits as on-call crew when a boat came up a person short.

He learned that it was a *thing* two years ago while hanging out at Fremont Brewing's Urban Beer Garden after a long day cutting code at Adobe. Their offices commanded the waterfront by the Fremont drawbridge.

At the next table, a couple were fighting about whose

turn it was to helm the boat in that night's race. Watching the summertime Tuesday Duck Dodge evening races out on Lake Union in the heart of Seattle was fun. But he'd never given any thought to being aboard, until the guy had stormed off and the woman looked around the bar like a lost soul. Short, cute, and curvy, they'd dated long enough for him to learn the basics of sailing and have a good laugh together. She let him and other volunteers crew every position, except the helm—that was hers alone now that she'd canned the fiancé.

Howie had quickly learned to read the local racing calendars and started making a few educated guesses. The Fremont Brewery or Duke's on Tuesday afternoons led to Duck Dodge slots. The bar at Ray's Boathouse the night before a race out of Shilshole turned out to be a great place to be picked up as last-minute crew. Laurelhurst had too much money to ever consider wanting crew like him, but Anthony's Homeport along the Kirkland waterfront was a consistent winner.

There were now a score of boat skippers with his number on speed dial. Two, even three races a week came his way almost year round. He'd never spent a dollar past his bar tab, one pint and an appetizer limit unless some winning captain was buying for the crew. There'd been no need to join any of the yacht clubs.

Except for missing the Christmas parties.

Despite his initial introduction, sailing women were in a special class all their own—rare. Men dominated the sport. Howie soon learned, however, that grown-daughters-of came out of the woodwork at special moments...like Christmas parties.

But he had to adhere to his policy of minimal expense. He was only about halfway to affording his own boat big enough to live aboard but fast enough to be fun. Or maybe even rigged for the ultimate: going deep sea. Circumnavigating. Hard to imagine but it sounded very cool. Until then? He'd stay focused on hitting those great holiday parties.

He'd built enough connections to enough different boats that he always heard about the various parties. This being the self-proclaimed sailing capital of the US of A, there were a lot of them. Between Halloween and the end of the Christmas boat parades on December 23rd was in many ways the peak of the sailing season—or at least the *social* sailing season.

But finding a date, even on a one-evening basis to attend a party, was tricky because the sailing women were so rare.

Then the great idea came. Who could turn away a gate-crashing Santa, even one with a Brooklyn-Jew accent?

3

Janine surveyed the yacht club decorations. Thank God last night's storm had played itself out, which would be a boon for attendance. She so didn't want to be the person who organized a party and no one came. From the crackling fire at one end of the hall to the giant Christmas tree at the other, it was beautiful.

"This is amazing! Great job!" Janine had to give credit where credit was due.

Bethany and her pair of BFFs offered her thankful smiles that didn't reach their steel-like eyes, but they *had* done well. And it had cost the club only fifty dollars.

In keeping with her Pirate's Christmas theme, the Queen Bethany Trio scrounged among the membership for old manila lines, wooden block-and-tackle, battered wooden chests, and the like. The tables, that Janine had insisted be set up in long communal-style rows over Georgina Anne's protests, were scattered with well-worn seafaring paraphernalia. The QBT had also raided various long-grown-children's toy boxes; rubber swords and daggers had been strewn about as well. Bethany had found nautical-chart paper tablecloths to spread along the tables, which had cost the fifty dollars and were sure to be conversation starters with any sailor.

Janine's personal playlist—of mixed sea shanties by the Cornish Fisherman's Friends group and Christmas carols—lent a cheery background.

Georgina Anne and Michael had eschewed festive wear beyond very conservative Christmas sweaters.

But not to be outdone by Janine's chosen theme, the QBT wore matching pirate maiden costumes that included high leather boots, alarmingly short skirts, and seriously low-cut bodices. Bandanas side-knotted as headbands allowed their latest hair styles to be on display while adding to the piratical air.

Courtesy of a brief fling several years ago that had overlapped Halloween, Janine possessed full Elizabeth Swann attire. Keira Knightley had rocked it in *Pirates of the Caribbean,* and their builds were similar enough that Janine had gone all in when putting it together—right down to the sheathed long sword dangling from a well-worn broad leather strap. Unsure why she could never throw it out, especially when space was always such a premium on a sailboat, she now knew. Without a word, simply by standing beside them, it changed the Queen Bethany Trio from sexy pirate maidens to cheap working girls in a pirate bar.

The fact was not lost on the BFFs, though Bethany pretended not to care. Of course, rumor said that Bethany was searching for a new *captain* for her personal boat, having divorced the second (or perhaps third) one two months ago. She appeared fully prepared to leverage all that the costume implied at the least hint of a major checking account.

Oddly, this was something relatively easy to assess in the boating community. Finding out the size and make of a person's sailboat, a natural conversation starter in a yachting club, quickly separated the pretenders and the wannabes from the truly affluent. A C&C 27 earned a scoff at best, though a J24 might command a little respect as it was a racer rather than a wallowing daysailer. Anything over fifty feet commanded attention. Her 41-foot boat floated in the murky middle ground, though it being a Cheoy Lee did earn her more attention than a longer Gulfstar or Cal might.

By the time of the official start of the potluck, the hall was already half full—a good turnout. About half had taken her challenge with costumes ranging from a simple bandana to a few other kits better than the QBT. Too bad she was judging the best costume competition, as so far she would be an easy win.

Her top choice so far was a family who had dressed as space pirates with obviously recycled astronaut Halloween costumes. They weren't incredible but the family absolutely owned it, especially the five-year-old girl brandishing her kid-sized red light saber.

Steaming pots and great platters of food soon had the buffet table groaning under the weight. Three sets of Swedish meatballs, several lasagnas, salads in every variety from Asian noodle to orange-cranberry. Two whole sides of salmon were sufficiently massive that even a concerted attack didn't kill them off until past the first hour. Not a single Jell-O salad—a staple of her Iowan youth—reared its ugly head.

The dessert table was like a light show: blueberry cobbler, a great sheet of golden baklava, the round eyes of orange pumpkin and lemon-yellow meringue pies were interspersed with M&M oatmeal cookies larger than her hand with the fingers spread.

Yet Janine could feel the change like a good skipper reading the winds before they wholly shifted and left your boat stranded on the wrong side of the course.

Second helpings tapered off. The dessert buffet slightly resembled the docks after a fish-cleaning session. An hour in and the event showed the first signs of fading. It was too early to start on the door prizes. The Spring Fling had revealed that this wasn't much of a dancing crowd. She cursed herself for not thinking up any games, probably because she'd always hated them when someone else did.

This evening was on the verge of winding down long before she was ready, considering all the effort and pain she'd put into the event. Desperate enough to approach the Queen Bethany Trio? Sadly, yes.

But when she went looking for them, she could only find the two BFFs.

"She's showing her boat to someone." The BFFs' shared look said that she wouldn't be back anytime soon. The Solaris 40 might be a foot shorter than her Cheoy Lee 41, but the interior was pure luxury. Bethany and her latest target might not resurface for days.

The BFFs were far more tolerable on their own, but

neither had any brilliant ideas to keep the party going either.

Maybe she should bow to the inevitable and start the door prizes early. Of course, with her luck, she'd then be accused of cutting short such a lovely evening. It was the no-win scenario with Captain Jack Sparrow nowhere in sight to rescue her. If she—

"Merry Christmas, ye blaggards!" The shout sliced through every conversation and focused all attention on the door.

4

"Heya! Heya! Heya! Can Santa make an entrance or what?"

It earned him a polite round of applause. Kinda middle ground. Not the polite patter from the Medina Yachters nor the round of cheers and a beer thudded on the bar before him at the Sloop Tavern.

He jumped up onto a table, brandishing the sword that he'd spiral wound with red-and-white electrical tape.

"Arrr! Come on people. Give Pirate Santa a proper arrr. ARRR!"

The response, especially from the kids and their families, improved by several levels. His little sister Stacey had been hyped on Broadway since seeing *The Lion King* at age six. She'd rarely been the lead in any school play, but she *always* nailed the scene-stealing comic relief. Good enough that this year Yale Drama gave her a major scholarship. For this event, he'd channel Stacey.

Howie flourished the hook clamped over his left hand. He'd picked it up at a local costume shop along with the sword, see-through eye patch, and tricorn hat. Though he'd never been *Pirate* Santa before, he couldn't resist the challenge when a buddy had forwarded him a copy of the invitation.

"ARRR!" he roared out again and the kids ate it up.

As he swashbuckled down the table, people yanked empty plates and glasses out of the way.

"So, who here has been a good lad or lassie—and who's been baaaad?"

A small voice popped up on cue. "I've been good," a pint-sized pirate with a raggedy shirt, a bandana, and an eyepatch flipped up.

"Good?" Howie blustered. "*Good?*"

He tucked his sword away and reached down to lift the little boy onto the table.

"I oughter make ya walk the gangplank. Less'n you was a-sayin' you were a good *pirate.*" He'd lost the kid, so Howie helped him out. "You been a good *pirate* for Pirate Santa, young lad?"

His sister had taught him that one of the keys was to dress the part. So, he'd done the full Santa fat suit and beard, and layered on the pirate with eyepatch, tricorn hat that he'd spray-painted bright red, and latex-makeup scars on the bits of cheek and forehead that showed. The other key, she'd insisted was to ham it up and never break character. So, he laid on the Brooklyn accent, the one he'd done his best to leave behind along with his youth, as thick as a Katz's pastrami on rye and dove into the pirate role.

"Yes, Pirate Santa."

"Well done, lad!" He unslung the red gift bag he'd

been wearing on a wide leather strap. Peeking inside, he found a Matchbox fire engine, the full ladder truck with the pivot in the middle, and handed it over. In moments, the pirate-in-training was once again in his chair, racing his new engine around the plate holding the last few bites of an apple pie.

"Har! Har! Har! Merry Christmas, lad!"

5

JANINE SLID OVER TO STAND BY GEORGINA ANN AND Michael. Now there was a match made in hell. Maybe she should push them together simply for the sheer spectacle. Of course, what if it worked? The vision dancing in her head of miniature versions of these two ruthlessly organizing the world was enough to stop the thought.

"Okay. Who hired the Pirate Santa from Brooklyn?"

They both shrugged. "We thought you did."

"It *is* rather crass," Georgina Ann continued. "Hadn't you already made a sufficient mockery of the event as it is?"

Michael was nodding his agreement.

"Gods, you two *do* belong together."

"We what?" they said in unison. Then they both looked at her before turning to inspect each other.

Crap! Now she really had unleashed the Christmas Gorgon or Hydra or whatever mythical monster it was that got released at Christmas.

Well, it *was* her event. Which meant whatever happened was up to her.

She moved up to Santa who'd returned to floor level as he dug deep into his bag for a little girl.

"Ah!" he spotted her. "Santa's Pirate Elf just when I needed her. Sit. Sit." He pointed at the floor.

Caught unawares, Janine sat cross-legged on the floor, placing her eye-to-eye with the little girl.

Santa fished out a stethoscope.

"Put these in your ears," he instructed the little girl as he helped her. "And you'll hear something amazing."

He handed the business end to Janine. Without any hint of risqué, the V-neck of her blouse still opened enough for her to place the pickup close above her left breast.

The girl's eyes shot wide.

"You can listen to anyone's heart," the Pirate Santa told her.

"Even Mr. Tom's?" she asked in an overloud voice.

He tickled the side of her ribs with the tip of his plastic hook. "When ye get home, lass, listen right there, just behind Mr. Tom's front leg on either side. And try right here on his throat," the hook touched the side of Janine's throat, "when he starts to purr. Do you purr?"

Janine hadn't expected the last to be addressed to her.

Snagging her wrist with his hook, he moved the stethoscope from above her breast to beside her throat.

She pressed the pickup there and did her best to purr.

The girl giggled in delight. "You don't sound nothing like Mr. Tom." Then the shyness kicked in. She leaned in to whisper to the man in the well-padded red-and-white suit that was at least as high quality as her own pirate outfit. "Thank you, Santa." The girl scurried away, clutching her stethoscope tightly to her chest.

"I hope she has a patient cat," Pirate Santa appeared to be grinning behind the fake white beard.

"Who—" But her attempt to ask who he was, and each subsequent attempt after that was cut off by the arrival of another child. He soon had a waiting crowd.

Each time, he listened carefully to them, asking questions. Then he'd fish around in his bag. Nothing was wrapped, nor was any of it new. Some showed signs of repair, touched-up paint and so on. But each gift delighted its recipient.

"How—"

She was as unsuccessful with that question as *Who.*

But during the quiet in-between moments, Santa explained. "Pirate Santa hits the thrift stores. Picks over the toy sections—"

"And the doctor ones," she interjected, realizing that the girl now owned a genuine stethoscope, not some imitation that would break before she could listen to her cat's heart.

"Sure. Marine stuff, farmer, chef—though no knives. Whatever comes to hand. Fix it up and give them away. It's a good goof, all in fun, dat fer sure. Pirate Santa and his pirate elf," he offered her a broad wink, "take care of his wee crewmates, dat's all o' the game." Only a lone eye was clearly visible, and one of the fake scars tugged the wink askew.

She'd swear that his Brooklyn accent grew thicker the longer she stayed near him. Janine was about to fade away, though not too far as he remained an unknown, when she caught onto the pattern of the gifts. Boys wanted the little cars and trucks along with the occasional action figures. For the girls, there were a few dolls, but most received a next-level gift like the stethoscope, a small hand telescope, or a children's book of knot-tying with a length of line. One of the older girls received a scientific calculator complete with a printed-off copy of the instruction manual.

That was what kept her closer than merely keeping an eye on him.

6

_____

HOWIE HAD BEEN FOLLOWING A ROUTINE THAT HE'D HONED a dozen or more times with great success. Though he'd never had an elf assistant before, especially not one who looked so incredible. At her first attempt to slip away, he placed the next little kid in her lap to keep her in place.

Long and sleek. Thick hair, the chocolatey brown of Santa's reindeer, flowed down over her shoulders and offered a glorious distraction. The low brim of her black tricorn hat shaded her eyes so that he couldn't see their color. And dressed in a costume that looked like it was straight out of the 1700s. She was utterly astonishing. Exactly the woman any pirate king would want by his side to make him the envy of all far and wide.

He set himself up on a chair on one of the tables and had her assisting *Those who sought an audience with Pirate Santa* to step up onto *Pirate Santa's throne.* She had the poise and build of a dancer, but demonstrated a surprising strength when handling even the stoutest boy or girl—a sailing pirate's strength for sure.

From up here, he could also judge the ebb and flow of the room. He could usually sustain this game for ten or fifteen minutes. It was over half an hour before he finally closed his bag for the last time. Then he stood and bowed to the four corners of the room, honoring the four winds. The applause was almost a roar, his best yet. He could see why his sister was so hyped on it, even if he never wanted to do it out of a Santa—or a Pirate Santa—suit.

Then he reached out a hand toward the lovely elf. Not down, but coaxing her up to stand on the table beside him.

Her blush shot bright, but she stepped on a wobbly chair with perfect surety and joined him aloft.

Then he took her hand, raised their joined grasp high, then swung it down. Only a bit off the cue, she took the indication to bow. The applause continued.

As it died away, he called out, "Santa sees there's still plenty o' fine desserts awaitin'. What kind of a pirate crew are ye to be leaving such vittles laying about?" It earned a laugh and turned the crowd's attention back to the buffet line.

The elf retrieved her hand and jumped lightly down from the table. But she didn't walk away. Instead, she held the chair steady for him. He was far less graceful in his heavy boots, fat suit, and a hook for a left hand.

"Party crasher?" she asked from mere inches away once he stood again on *terra firma*. Her eyes were the color of a darkening sky, but he didn't see any storm brewing there.

"What else would ye expect from a Pirate Santa?"

"Far less than this one has earned tonight." She kissed

him on the cheek above his white beard but below the latex scar that was squinting up his exposed eye—a mistake he'd never make again as it was seriously annoying.

By the end of the evening, Howie knew several things.

First, the elfin pirate had almost no skills with people. She was as forthright as her pirate attire suggested. While she didn't offend, she was crap at superficial chit-chat. He recognized it as a trait they absolutely shared.

Second, she was organized enough to lead an entire pirate rabble to victory. The whole evening finished smoothly. Including the family of space pirates winning best group costume and a gift certificate to the Museum of Science.

Third, he remained his usual awkward real-life self despite being the Pirate Santa. He departed well-fed and thanked—without discovering her name or asking for her phone number.

Fourth, he was completely gone on the woman who had set a whole new standard for attractive piratical elves.

7

THE CHRISTMAS SHIP PARADE OF BOATS WAS ALWAYS A
tricky challenge. Tourists paid top dollar to ride on the
Argosy tour boat with fine cocktails, appetizers, and a
caroling choir. No self-respecting Seattle boat skipper
would be caught dead on such a cruise—or paying that
much money for a ninety-minute outing.

However, it was the lead ship on the final night of the
parade of boats dressed up in Christmas lights. On
evenings throughout December, there were parades
along different sections of Seattle's waterfront—
something the city boasted a lot of. But December 23rd
counted as the big one and she'd hate to miss it.

Janine had sailed every parade this year, and after
going to so much trouble dressing up *Tārā*, she'd hate
missing the final one. But her normal call-up crew felt
that their office Christmas party was more important. She
hoped that they told the truth about having to put in an
appearance, rather than what she suspected—that they'd

have more fun at their office than with her. Personally, she was always happiest alone on her boat.

She could single-hand *Tārā* in all conditions except for the busiest of races. But passing solo through the Ballard Locks was just begging for trouble. She moored at Shilshole Marina on Puget Sound, and tonight's cruise was along the Lake Union waterfront, five miles and one tricky set of locks away.

A few calls up and down the docks to the other liveaboards revealed they were having similar crew problems. Alice and Jake gave her a number to try. *He's a good hand, dead reliable. Decent guy.*

Her excitement about inviting a strange guy onto her boat for a six-hour cruise ranked mighty low. But when, six calls later, Quint gave her the same number, she caved.

A couple quick texts and she had her crew, for better or worse.

At T dock, pinged into her phone.

Janine glared at the text, then ponytailed her hair under her hoodie and pulled on a windbreaker. It was a good night, calm and dead clear, which meant chilly headed for downright cold. Sure enough, by the time she reached the head of the dock to open the security gate, she had to snug down the hoodie and was wishing for a mug of hot chocolate.

Though he was silhouetted by the parking lot lights behind him, the guy on the other side of the wire mesh didn't look dangerous. His height was all she could really tell, a few inches over hers. A cable-knit orange wool hat was tugged down to his eyebrows. A multi-colored scarf around his neck, and the heavy jacket said he knew what he was getting into. He was carrying a satchel.

"What have you got there?"

"My standard kit, though I hope I don't need it tonight: inflatable life vest, slicks, and a change of clothes."

"Okay." She opened the gate.

"There's also a dozen cookies from Dahlia Bakery in Belltown."

"You're hired."

He had a good laugh. Down at Slip T19 he came to a halt. "Is this a Cheoy Lee?"

"The 41." Janine was more than a little charmed. It was unusual enough that not many could pick one out of a crowd. "Her name is *Tārā.*" She liked the way he scanned the boat. Not wide-eyed neophyte, but rather pausing only briefly as he cataloged the deck layout, line paths, and tiedowns.

"You don't strike me as the sort to be burning down the South."

Everyone always assumed that her boat was named for Scarlett's plantation in *Gone with the Wind.* Even if they saw the odd spelling, which this guy couldn't without going to the stern and bending down to look.

"Uh, I never got your name."

"Howie."

"Hi, I'm Janine. Thanks for lending a hand tonight."

"Always glad of a chance to cruise in the Christmas parades." He tossed his bag inside the lifelines.

She hopped aboard. "*Tārā* was a female Buddha or a bodhisattva, depending on who you talk to. She's the

Mother of Liberation. Success in work and achievements also fall under her purview." She started the engine.

"Cool! Liberation from the hum-drum life. I like it." Howie caught the end of the spring line after she untied it, flipped it off the dock cleat and tossed it aboard forward in a neat coil. Without needing any prompting, he untied the stern line, left a loop over the dock cleat, and handed her the loose end. That would let her keep the boat in place until she was actively backing out of the slip. Finally he undid the bow line and stood ready to walk the boat out.

No questioning his familiarity with proper line work.

In minutes they were sliding through the night waters. He clipped the safety lines securely, then cleared the rubber bumpers that had dangled off the side between the boat and the dock. He continued until he'd dressed all the lines as neatly as she always did.

After snagging his bag, he hesitated at the head of the companionway down into the boat.

She waved him ahead as she navigated her way along the back of the Shilshole breakwater. Manners too. Who was this guy?

8

Howie didn't want Janine to think he was snooping; the woman came across as seriously serious. He'd intended to toss his bag on a bunk and return to the deck immediately, but the interior required a good long look.

She was no simple daysailer—neither the woman nor the boat.

There were obvious signs that not only did Janine live aboard, but that her boat was capable of far more serious adventures than a parade of Christmas lights. The instruments at the chart were top quality gear. Not merely an ICOM two-way, but also a handheld and a satellite radio. The GPS and navigation equipment was sufficiently impressive that he'd want a good long spell with the instruction manual before approaching it.

And the interior. Janine was a very practical woman. There were only hints here and there as to the owner's gender. But she had a fantastic physical library of the great mariners from Bligh to Chichester. There were also travel guides that appeared to include most major countries with a coastline. A slim set of volumes about Arctic and Antarctic exploration were particularly intriguing.

Too long below, though the thoroughly efficient and comfortable interior tempted him to linger, he turned to ascend the ladder to the deck.

Except his way was blocked. Sitting there at the base of the ladder, a large black-and-white cat regarded him suspiciously.

"What's his or her name?" he called up to Janine loudly enough to be heard over the engine rumble as he knelt to let the cat sniff his hand.

"He. Ship's Captain Master Howl. Be sure to salute."

He glanced up the ladder at her. What little of her face he could see between the hoodie and the darkness showed no sign she was joking. So, he knelt as straight as he could, then saluted sharply before reaching out to pet him. The cat had a ready purr.

Howie scooped him up and carried Master Howl up to join his mistress above decks.

"Now you're spoiling him rotten." She showed the first hint of humor since his arrival.

"And you don't? You made him ship's captain."

"Oh no, he did that on his own. I merely bowed to the inevitable. Here, take the wheel." And she simply walked away from him.

In all his sailing, it was the one thing he did the very least—as in never. It was part of how he'd fit into every crew, by never going for the wheel or tiller.

She disappeared below.

The steel wheel radiated cold against his palms, cold

enough it almost burned. But he didn't dare let go to fish out his gloves. Instead, he held on for dear life and did his best to stay on track for the opening at the south end of Shilshole and the turn into Salmon Bay and the locks.

Foolishly trusting him, Janine stayed below forever— at least a minute, perhaps two. Other boats were coming out of darkened docks. Picking their running lights out of their extravagant Christmas finery was tricky.

Then she must have thrown a breaker and the *Tārā's* lights blinked on. Which was a massive understatement. The boat glittered with a galaxy of multi-colored lights. After that, everyone stayed out of his way as if he was Neptune, God of the Sea.

She finally reappeared, only to set down a pair of bowls on the floor of the cockpit. Master Howl thumped down from the seat he'd been lounging on and began eating his dinner.

Then Janine was back out of sight, reappearing only to set out a big thermos, then two mugs, and finally his box of cookies.

When she returned to the deck, she didn't take the wheel. Instead, she sat on one of the side seats and filled the two thermal travel mugs from the thermos.

"Hope hot chocolate's okay. I can't drink coffee past the first cup of the morning or I end up more jittery than Master Howl." As her cat seemed more likely to yawn than jitter, he wasn't terribly worried.

"Hot chocolate born and bred." He accepted the mug and managed the turn into Salmon Bay without crashing her boat into a channel buoy. A minor triumph in his opinion.

He could feel her eyes on him. "What's wrong?"

"I've never taken the helm before."

"Never? Why?"

He shrugged, though that probably didn't show through his heavy parka. "Earned my first ride as crew because of a couple fighting over control of the helm while they were still ashore. Figured my best way to keep sailing was to keep my hands off."

"But the rest of it?" She waved a gloved hand at the rest of the boat.

"A hundred and thirty-seven races from winch grinder to foredeck sail handler."

"Over hard right!" She snapped out.

He didn't see a reason but wasn't going to mess with that tone. He looked right to make sure no one was in the channel beside him and turned the wheel to starboard.

"Spin it! All the way!"

So he did through two full turns until the wheel hit a stop with a solid *thunk!* he could feel through his palms. The boat turned like it was dancing.

"Back the other way!"

He spun back to port, four turns until the wheel thunked against the other stop. The boat spun with equal agility in the other direction.

"Settle straight up the channel," her voice turned utterly patient.

She sat in silence as he tried but overcorrected one way and then the other before he found the center position again *and* had them headed in the right direction.

"That gives you a beginning feel for how she handles, agile without being twitchy."

And that set the tone for the evening.

She handled lines, but never touched the wheel or the engine controls. Instead, she offered clear, precise instructions on boat handling and then explained what he was feeling as he did so.

"Put the engine in neutral and feel how she coasts. Twelve-six beam on a forty-one-foot hull weighing twelve tons fully loaded, she glides longer than you'd expect. Skeg keel, so if you nudge it into reverse, she only walks a little to the left."

He put it into reverse and, as they slowed, the bow did indeed swing to the left, but was easily corrected with a light turn of the wheel.

9

———

TWENTY-TWO FEET UP THROUGH THE BUSIEST SET OF LOCKS in the entire US, she kept a hawk eye on Howie, ready to leap in at the least provocation. But he tended to under- rather than over-control, which was a pleasant change and avoided the most common mistakes.

He learned incredibly quickly. It made sense once she thought about it. She typically set neophyte friends at the helm to get a feel for a boat. It was strange to have someone who was an experienced sailor in every way *except* steering.

Howie's attempts to relinquish control tapered off as he became more and more used to how the boat reacted. In her early days, she'd had to fight for even moments at a boat's helm, until she was so fed up that she'd bought her own. Janine had long ago sworn that she'd never be one of *those* skippers.

And if she were to take Howie at his word, he wasn't one of those control-freak-effing-asshole guys either.

They slid along the Washington Ship Canal in the

company of the other eight boats that had been in their same lift through the locks. Others were joining them from the commercial yards to either side of the passage.

As they emerged into Lake Union, Howie lost all control. She didn't take the helm away from him, but did stretch out a foot without disturbing Master Howl in her lap and nudged the throttle back to idle.

"Holy shit!"

She could only smile. There were some experiences he clearly hadn't had. The various boat parades typically included twenty boats. This final-night gathering on Lake Union, in the northern heart of Seattle downtown, was an outright extravaganza.

Argosy Cruises had all three of their big tourist boats out and lit up like birthday cakes. Several boats in the hundred-foot-plus class floated like pylons in the middle of the lake for the other boats to swirl around. Powerboats abounded, from tiny skiffs to luxury yachts.

Sailboats stood out clearly because most had a string of lights that traced from the stern, up the mast's backstay to the peak, then down the forestay to the bow. Others enhanced that with a string of lights down the mast so that it looked as if their sails were up with edges alight.

Not quite sure why, Janine had gone a little crazy this year. She'd run lights up every shroud and sidestay, and wound around the main boom. More lights outlined the edge where deck met hull and others traced the top of the cabin. She'd done it all with colored LED twinkle lights so the cockpit itself remained shrouded in near darkness, but *Tārā* glittered.

A hundred or more boats littered the water, providing

a kaleidoscopic ever-shifting light show. Hers was a standout, drawing applause from those ashore every time they drifted close.

And somehow in that moment, she understood what she'd been doing as if everything suddenly, finally made sense. *Tārā*, the Mistress of Liberation, had been setting her up for a long time without her being aware of it.

Like breaking through a bank of fog, the course she'd been sailing was so clear now that she could see it.

First, her entire library had gone digital, *except* for the tales of the great explorers and circumnavigators.

Then, she'd collected travel guides simply for the fun of imagining what was out there.

Third, *Tārā's* gear and sail-set were utterly ridiculous for kicking around Puget Sound—but perfect for heading off deep sea.

Even her job, she'd shifted to online and lately focused strictly on contract piecework. Log in, get it done, get paid, and move on.

It would have been nice to have someone to voyage with. Some part of her had kept her plans on hold, out of her own sight, but to no avail. In three years of waiting, she hadn't found the right fit once. Someone both serious and funny—the first to put up with her and the latter to lighten her up a little. She'd certainly heard that diagnosis from enough exes to believe it necessary. They had to be smart, independent, adventurous...

Yeah, her cat was, sadly, as close as she'd ever come.

Officially sick of waiting, only one question remained. *When?*

Spring. Once the winter storms had abated, she'd head out. March, April at the latest.

And that's why she'd ultra-decorated this Christmas. She, *Tārā*, and Master Howl were saying goodbye to Seattle with far more style and flair than she usually managed in her day-to-day life.

She looked down at Master Howl.

"If we're off to conquer the high seas, I should have worn my pirate outfit."

10

"YOUR *WHAT?*" HOWIE HADN'T MEANT TO SHOUT. HE suddenly had the undivided attention of every sailor within a dozen boat-lengths, as well the party currently rocking out on the Ivar's Restaurant barge.

Janine had gone quiet for the last twenty minutes or so, leaving it up to him to slowly adapt to navigating an unfamiliar boat through such heavy traffic. His nerves had finally pushed him to the far quieter northeast corner of Lake Union near Ivar's.

The Number 12 red marker buoy below the I-5 overpass bridge was a common turning point for summertime Duck Dodge races and he knew it well. He'd been using that to practice various turns as he learned more of how the boat handled under power. It would be very different under sail and he'd love to learn that too.

The parts of his mind that weren't occupied with learning were busy debating the best way to ask Janine if she needed a regular crew. Maybe she'd let him try the helm under sail.

And then she'd spoken—to herself and her cat—but with the engine barely above an idle her voice had carried clearly.

"Your…" he tried to catch his breath. There was no way. She was several inches shorter than the woman who'd been stuck in his mind for the two weeks since he'd played the Pirate Santa. He'd considered breaking his rule and joining the yacht club simply to find her.

"My what?" She looked up at him. There were enough work lights in the nearby boatyard that he had his first really clear look at her face.

"Your…pirate outfit?" It was to be her.

She looked away—exactly as she had when he'd beckoned her to take her bow on the tabletop. "It's silly."

That's when he remembered her stepping so lightly on the chair to climb up on the table beside him. Her leather pirate boots had several inches of stout heel. It was her.

He considered not saying anything. *Oh, hi. I crashed your yacht-club party once, acting like a total lunatic. By the way, I think I may love you.*

Not a good start.

I've had this huge fantasy crush on you since…

Please let me bow at your feet, my pirate elf.

Yeah, a fast track course for a cold swim to shore.

And she thought that *she* was the one who'd been silly?

"Tell me," he eased the boat to port to avoid ramming a Christmas canoe that had twinkle lights twisted around the paddles. They even wore black outfits so that only the paddles showed. "I'll bet I can out-foolish you."

She shook her head and kept her silence.

"C'mon," he knew he was pleading, "how am I supposed to talk you into teaching me how to really sail if you won't tell me the embarrassing shit?"

She turned to face him, studying him in that quiet way he couldn't believe he hadn't recognized earlier.

"Okay. This is going to sound beyond stupid."

"I can out-do it. I swear on Master Howl's food bowl." That earned him a brief smile.

"I was recently in charge of a Pirate Christmas party. And there was this guy." Again one of those vast silences that shouted so loudly about who she was.

"I hate him already."

"He crashed the party as, you're not going to believe this, a Pirate Santa. He was loud, ridiculous—"

And curling up to die at the helm of your boat.

"—and probably the most decent guy I've met in years."

11

HOWIE HAD GONE STRANGELY QUIET UNTIL THEY'D returned down through the Ballard Locks and had retied the boat at Shilshole. The only thing she could figure out was he must now deem her to be a total idiot. Who ever would get a crush on a Pirate Santa whose face she'd never seen.

His silence had let her dredge up thoughts she hadn't found in the last two weeks since the events of that night. And she let them out, tales told into the chill night.

The way he treated those kids.

With simple gifts, he gave those girls lofty visions of what they could be.

Without her realizing it, he'd sailed into her thoughts as smoothly as *Tārā* slicing through a wave. He'd been too loud and brash for her, and his Brooklyn accent had often grown almost incomprehensibly thick to her Iowan ear. But he'd...well, she'd liked him.

And the idea of finally heading out to cross the seas was so big and fresh that it too had spilled out of her. The

M. L. BUCHMAN

fantasy of sailing from one exotic place to another, seeing the world. Making some money when she hit a port and could connect in; she owned her own floating home, so the costs were low and she could carry on for...years.

And why she'd dumped all of that on Howie still mystified her. He'd been quiet and listened. Somehow he made it okay for her to speak the thoughts she never said to anyone, not even Master Howl. Or herself.

It was only as they were tying off the spring line on the boat and plugging in the shore-power cable that she realized something. He'd convinced her to give him sailing lessons next weekend. And even made a tentative date for New Year's Eve if they went well.

But... "Hey, you never told me how you could *out-foolish* me."

Howie stood in the darkness beside her on the dock. The temperature had dropped enough that their breath issued as white clouds. By that alone, she could see that he'd tipped his head back to stare up at the stars.

They were crystal bright, at least for being so close to the parking lot and the low wash lights that lit the dock's planking. From deep sea? A thousand miles from the next nearest light? Janine couldn't wait to see them.

"Well, I'm not sure how to say this."

"Try." She'd laid out every ridiculous dream she had and needed someone, anyone, to tell her it wasn't a pile of steaming hooey, even this near stranger.

Howie leaned back against the hull of her boat, which drifted away from the dock, almost enough to plop his butt down into the water before the lines snubbed it to a halt. Once he stood squarely on the dock again, he let out a big cloud of breath, then turned to face her.

"Your dream is beyond beautiful, Janine. I can't find a way of saying how much I want to do it with you without sounding like a total stalker."

And he saw he was right as Janine shifted a step back along the dock.

Howie reached out a hand to stop her, but withdrew it before he touched her. He *so* wanted to touch her.

"Except maybe this..."

"What?" she asked when he didn't continue.

He took hope from how she'd described him and dug deep for his best Brooklyn-Jew-pirate, and spoke softly...

"Arrrr! The lovely Pirate Queen needs a Pirate Santa in her life, don't she?"

———

If you enjoyed this story
please consider leaving a review.
They really help.

Keep reading for an exciting excerpt from:
Where Dreams #1: *Where Dreams are Born*

WHERE DREAMS ARE BORN (EXCERPT)

IF YOU ENJOYED THAT, YOU'LL LOVE THIS TALE!

WHERE DREAMS ARE BORN
(EXCERPT)

RUSSELL LEANED HIS BACK AGAINST THE STUDIO DOOR after he locked it behind the last of the staff. He barely managed the energy to turn off his camera.

He knew it was good. The images were there; he'd really captured them.

But something was missing.

The groove ran so clean when he slid into it. First his Manhattan high-ceilinged loft would fade into the background, then the strobe lights, reflector umbrellas, and green-screen backdrops all became texture and tone.

Image, camera, and man then became one and nothing else mattered—a single flow of light, beginning before time was counted, and ending its journey in the printed image. One ray of primordial light traveling forever to glisten off the BMW roadster still parked in one corner of the rough-planked wood floor worn smooth by generations of use. Another ray lost in the dark blackness of the finest leather bucket seats. A hundred more picking out the supermodel's perfect hand dangling a single shining and golden key—the image shot just slow enough that the key blurred as it spun, but the logo remained clear.

He couldn't quite put his finger on it...

It would be another great ad by Russell Morgan, Inc. The client would be knocked dead—the ad leaving all others standing still as it roared down the passing lane. This one might get him another Clio, or even a second Mobius.

But...

There wasn't usually a "but."

And there definitely wasn't supposed to be one.

The groove had definitely been there, but he hadn't been in it.

That was the problem. It had slid along, sweeping his staff into their own orchestrated perfection, but he'd remained untouched. That ideal, seamless flow hadn't included him at all.

"Be honest, boyo, that session sucked," he told the empty studio. Everything had come together so perfectly for yet another ad for yet another high-end glossy. *Man, the Magazine* would launch spectacularly in a few weeks, a high-profile mid-December launch, and it would include a never before seen twelve-page spread by the great Russell Morgan. The rag would probably never pay off the lavish launch party of hope, ice sculptures, and chilled magnums of champagne before disappearing like a thousand before it.

"Morose much?"

The studio kept its thoughts to itself—the first reliable sign that he wasn't totally losing his shit.

He stowed the last camera with the others piled by his computer. At the breaker box he shut off the umbrellas, spots, scoops, and washes. The studio shifted from a stark landscape in hard-edged relief to a nest of curious shadows and rounded forms. The tang of hot metal and deodorant were the only lasting result of the day's efforts.

"Get your shit together, Russell." His reflection in the darkened window, stories above the streetlights of West 10th, was unimpressed and proved it was wise enough to not answer back. There was never a "down" after a shoot; there was always an "up."

Not tonight.

He'd kept everyone late—even though it was Thanksgiving eve—hoping for that smooth slide of image-camera-man. It was only when he saw the power of the images he captured that he knew he wasn't a part of the chain anymore and decided he'd paid enough triple-time expenses.

The next to last two-page spread would be the killer —shot with the door open against a background as black as the sports car's finish, the model's single perfect leg wrapped in thigh-high red-leather boots all that was visible in the driver's seat. The sensual juxtaposition of woman and sleek machine served as an irresistible focus. It was an ad designed to wrap every person with even a hint of a Y-chromosome around its little finger. And those with only X-chromosomes would simply want to be her. He'd shot a perfect combo of sex for the guys and power for the women.

Even the final one-page image, a close-up of driver's seat from exactly the same angle, revealing not the model but instead a single rose of precisely the same hue as the leather boot, hadn't moved him despite its perfection.

Without him noticing, Russell had become no more than the observer, merely a technician behind the camera. Now that he faced it, months, maybe even a year had passed since he'd been yanked all the way into the light-image-camera-man slipstream. Tonight was a wakeup call and he didn't like it one bit. Wakeup calls happened to others, not him. But tonight he could no longer ignore it, he hadn't even trailed along in the churned-up wake.

"You're just a creative cog in the advertising machine." Ouch! That one stung, but it didn't turn aside the relentless steamroller of his thoughts speeding down some empty, godforsaken autobahn.

His career was roaring ahead, his business' growth running fast and smooth. But, now that he considered it, he really didn't give a damn.

His life looked perfect, but—"Don't think it!"—his autobahn mind finished despite the command, *it wasn't*.

Russell left his silent reflection to its own thoughts and went through the back door that led to his apartment —closing it tightly on the perfect BMW, the perfect rose, and somewhere, lost among a hundred other props from dozens of other shoots, the long pair of perfect red-leather Chanel boots that had been wrapped around the most expensive legs in Manhattan. He didn't care if he never walked back through that door again. He'd been doing his art by rote; how god-awful sad was that?

And just to rub salt in the wound, he shot *commercial* art.

He'd never had the patience to do art for art's sake. Delayed gratification was his idea of no fun at all. He left the apartment dark with only the city's soft glow through the blind-covered windows revealing the vaguest outlines of the framed art on the wall. Even that almost overwhelmed him tonight.

He didn't want to see the huge prints by the *art* artists: autographed Goldsworthy, Liebowitz, and Joseph Francis' photomosaics for the moderns. A hundred and fifty rare, even one-of-a-kind prints adorned his walls—all the way back through Bourke-White to Russell's prize, an original Daguerre. The Museum of Modern Art kept begging to borrow his collection for a show...and at the moment he was half tempted to dump the whole lot in their Dumpster if they didn't want it.

Crossing the one-room loft apartment—as spacious as the studio—he bypassed the circle of avant-garde chairs that were almost as uncomfortable as they looked and avoided the lush black-leather wrap-around sectional sofa of such ludicrous scale that it could be a playpen for two or host a party for twenty. He cracked the fridge in the stainless-steel-and-black corner kitchen searching for something other than his usual beer.

A bottle of Krug.

Maybe he was just being grouchy after a long day's work.

Juice.

No. He'd run his enthusiasm into the ground but good.

Milk even.

Would he miss the camera if he never picked it up again?

No reaction.

Nothing.

Not even an itch in his palm.

That was an emptiness he did not want to face. Especially not alone, in his apartment, in the middle of the world's most vibrant city.

Russell turned away, and just as the door swung closed, the last sliver of light—the relentless chilly blue-white of the refrigerator bulb—shone across his bed. A quick grab snagged the edge of the door and left the narrow beam illuminating a long pale form on his black-silk bedspread.

The Chanel boots weren't in the studio after all. They were still wrapped around those three thousand dollar-an-hour legs: the only clothing on a perfect body. Five foot-eleven of intensely toned female anatomy right down to an exquisitely stair-mastered behind. Her long, white-blonde hair lay as a perfect Godiva over her tanned breasts—except for their too exact symmetry, even the closest inspection didn't reveal the work done there. She lay with one leg raised just ever so slightly to hide what was meant to be revealed later.

Melanie.

By the steady rise and fall of her flat stomach, he knew she'd fallen asleep while waiting for him to finish in the studio.

How long had they been an item? Two months? Three?

She'd made him feel alive...at least when he was

actually with her. Melanie was the super-model in his bed or on his arm at yet another SoHo gallery opening. Together they journeyed to sharp parties and trendy three-star restaurants where she dazzled and wooed yet another gathering of New York's finest with her ever so soft, so sensual, and so studied French accent. Together they were wired into the heart of the in-crowd.

But that wasn't him, was it? It didn't sound like the Russell he once knew.

Perhaps "they" were about how *he* looked on *her* arm?

Did she know tomorrow was the annual Thanksgiving ordeal at his parents? The grand holiday gathering that he'd rather die than attend? Any number of eligible woman would be floating about his parents' house out in Greenwich; anyone able to finagle an invitation would attend in hopes of snaring one of *People Magazine's* "100 Most Eligible." They all wanted to land the heir to a billion or some such; though he was wealthy enough on his own, by his own sweat, to draw anyone's attention. He ranked number twenty-four on the list this year—up from forty-seven the year before despite Tom Cruise being available yet again.

But not Melanie. He knew that it wasn't the money that drew her. Yes, she wanted him. But even more, she wanted the life that came with him—wrapped in the man-package. She wanted The Life. The one that *People Magazine* readers dreamed about between glossy pages.

His fingertips were growing cold where they held the refrigerator door cracked open.

If he woke her there'd be amazing sex. Or a great party to go to. Or...

Did he want "Or"? What more did he want from her?

Sex. Companionship. An energy, a vivacity, a thirst he feared that he lacked. Yes.

But where was that smooth synchronicity hiding, like the light-image-camera-man of photography that he'd lost? Where lurked that perfect flow from one person to another? Did she feel it? Could he ever feel it? Did it even exist?

"More?" he whispered into the darkness to test the sound. He knew all about wanting more.

The refrigerator door slid shut—escaping from his numbed fingers—which plunged the apartment back into darkness, taking Melanie along with it.

His breath echoed in the vast darkness. Proof that he was alive if nothing more.

It was time to close the studio—time to be done with Russell Incorporated.

Then what?

Maybe Angelo would know what to do. He always claimed that he did. Maybe this time Russell would actually listen to his almost-brother, though he knew from the experience of being himself for the last thirty years that was unlikely.

Seattle.

Damn! He'd have to go to bloody Seattle to find his best friend. There was a possible upside to such a trip—maybe there'd be a flight out before tomorrow's mess at his parents'. He slapped his pocket, but once again he'd set his phone down in some unknown corner of the studio and it would take forever to find. He really needed two—one chained down so that he could always find it to call the other.

Russell considered the darkness. He could guarantee that Seattle wouldn't be a big hit with Melanie.

Now if he only knew whether that was a good thing or bad.

————

Keep reading now!
A great tale of romance and adventure,
Of sailboats, food, fashion, and fun.
Available at fine retailers everywhere.
Where Dreams are Born

And please don't forget that review for
Santa and the Pirate Queen.

ABOUT THE AUTHOR

USA Today and Amazon #1 Bestseller M. L. "Matt" Buchman has 70+ action-adventure thriller and military romance novels, 100 short stories, and lotsa audiobooks. PW says: "Tom Clancy fans open to a strong female lead will clamor for more." Booklist declared: "3X Top 10 of the Year." A project manager with a geophysics degree, he's designed and built houses, flown and jumped out of planes, solo-sailed a 50' sailboat, and bicycled solo around the world...and he quilts. More at: www. mlbuchman.com.

Other works by M. L. Buchman: *(* - also in audio)*

Action-Adventure Thrillers

Dead Chef
One Chef!
Two Chef!

Miranda Chase
Drone*
Thunderbolt*
Condor*
Ghostrider*
Raider*
Chinook*
Havoc*
White Top*
Start the Chase*
Lightning*

Science Fiction / Fantasy

Deities Anonymous
Cookbook from Hell: Reheated
Saviors 101

Single Titles
Monk's Maze
the Me and Elsie Chronicles

Contemporary Romance

Eagle Cove
Return to Eagle Cove
Recipe for Eagle Cove
Longing for Eagle Cove
Keepsake for Eagle Cove

Love Abroad
Heart of the Cotswolds: England
Path of Love: Cinque Terre, Italy

Where Dreams
Where Dreams are Born
Where Dreams Reside
Where Dreams Are of Christmas*
Where Dreams Unfold
Where Dreams Are Written
Where Dreams Continue

Non-Fiction

Strategies for Success
Managing Your Inner Artist/Writer
Estate Planning for Authors*
Character Voice
Narrate and Record Your Own
Audiobook*

Short Story Series by M. L. Buchman:

Action-Adventure Thrillers

Dead Chef

Miranda Chase Origin Stories

Romantic Suspense

Antarctic Ice Fliers

US Coast Guard

Contemporary Romance

Eagle Cove

Other

Deities Anonymous (fantasy)

Single Titles

The Emily Beale Universe
(military romantic suspense)

The Night Stalkers
MAIN FLIGHT
The Night Is Mine
I Own the Dawn
Wait Until Dark
Take Over at Midnight
Light Up the Night
Bring On the Dusk
By Break of Day
Target of the Heart
Target Lock on Love
Target of Mine
Target of One's Own
NIGHT STALKERS HOLIDAYS
Daniel's Christmas*
Frank's Independence Day*
Peter's Christmas*
Christmas at Steel Beach
Zachary's Christmas*
Roy's Independence Day*
Damien's Christmas*
Christmas at Peleliu Cove

Henderson's Ranch
Nathan's Big Sky*
Big Sky, Loyal Heart*
Big Sky Dog Whisperer*
Tales of Henderson's Ranch*

Shadow Force: Psi
At the Slightest Sound*
At the Quietest Word*
At the Merest Glance*
At the Clearest Sensation*

White House Protection Force
Off the Leash*
On Your Mark*
In the Weeds*

Firehawks
Pure Heat
Full Blaze
Hot Point*
Flash of Fire*
Wild Fire
SMOKEJUMPERS
Wildfire at Dawn*
Wildfire at Larch Creek*
Wildfire on the Skagit*

Delta Force
Target Engaged*
Heart Strike*
Wild Justice*
Midnight Trust*

Emily Beale Universe Short Story Series
The Night Stalkers
The Night Stalkers Stories
The Night Stalkers CSAR
The Night Stalkers Wedding Stories
The Future Night Stalkers

Delta Force
Th Delta Force Shooters
The Delta Force Warriors

Firehawks
The Firehawks Lookouts
The Firehawks Hotshots
The Firebirds

White House Protection Force
Stories

Future Night Stalkers
Stories (Science Fiction)

SIGN UP FOR M. L. BUCHMAN'S NEWSLETTER TODAY